BRYAN LEE O'MALLEY'S

PILG
VS THE

RIM
TM
WORLD

edited by James Lucas Jones | design by Bryan Lee O'Malley & Keith Wood

Published by Fourth Estate

Originally published in 2005 in the United States by Oni Press
www.onipress.com

First published in Great Britain in 2010 by
Fourth Estate
An imprint of HarperCollins*Publishers*
77–85 Fulham Palace Road
London W6 8JB
www.4thestate.co.uk
www.scottpilgrim.com

9

ISBN: 978-0-00-734048-4

Printed and bound in Great Britian by
Clays Ltd, St Ives plc

WHAT IS THIS?
SCOTT PILGRIM
TRANSFER STUDENT
16 YEARS OLD

ST. JOEL'S
CATHOLIC HIGH SCHOOL
NORTHERN ONTARIO
7 YEARS AGO
THIS IS WHERE YOU GET YOUR EDUCATION.
ARE YOU GUYS SERIOUS?
...

I CAN'T BELIEVE THIS!
LET'S GO!

PRINCIPAL

WHAT ARE YOU IN FOR?

6 The new kid

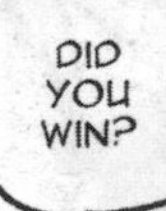

WELL, AT LEAST YOU'RE HONEST. ARE YOU NEW?
YEAH.
ME, TOO. I'M LISA.
SCOTT PILGRIM.
HOW LONG HAVE YOU BEEN HERE?
FIFTEEN MINUTES.
AND YOU ALREADY GOT BEAT UP? YOU MUST BE TOTALLY GREAT.
WE SHOULD BE FRIENDS.
YEAH?
UH-HUH.

SCOTT!
WHAT?
VISITOR!
WHAT? WHAT-EVER!
HEY!
WELL, HE'S OBVI-OUSLY DOWN THERE. JUST GO ON.
I DON'T EVEN KNOW ANYONE IN THIS TOWN!
COAL

WHAT ARE YOU DOING IN MY HOUSE??
NOT ACTUALLY LOOKING
YOUR BROTHER LET ME IN.
THIS IS RIDICULOUS! NO, WE CAN'T BE FRIENDS!
COAL
ARE YOU PLAYING VIDEO GAMES? DO YOU HAVE ANY LEMONADE?
YES! AND NO!
WE ONLY HAVE ICED TEA.
I'LL ASK YOUR BROTHER WHERE THE GLASSES ARE.
WHAT'S HIS NAME?
LAWRENCE. WHO ARE YOU?

FOODS
HEY! DO YOU KNOW THIS? HAVE YOU READ THIS?
WHAT? NO!
ENGLISH IS NEXT PERIOD, EH?
STOP IT! GO AWAY!
(HATES BEING BOTHERED WHEN EATING)
HAVE YOU EVER BOUGHT THESE MEXICAN FRIES? ISN'T THAT, LIKE... RACIST OR SOMETHING?
MY MOM PACKS MY LUNCH.
WHAT A SWEET, INNOCENT BOY YOU ARE.

BLUEBIR
NES
HEY.
HEY.
DO YOU HATE ME?

WHO IS "LISA MILLER?"
SCOTT'S GIRL-FRIEND.
SHE'S NOT MY GIRL-FRIEND!!!
LAWRENCE! SUPPER!!
YAP YAP YAP YAP
SCOTT, YOU HAVE A GIRLFRIEND? IS SHE CUTE?
YEAH, SCOTT, TELL US ALL ABOUT HER!
YAP YAP YAP
SHE'S NOT MY GIRLFRIEND!! I BARELY EVEN KNOW HER!!
LAWRENCE!! RIGHT NOW!!
YAP YAP YAP
DO YOU WANT HER TO BE YOUR GIRL-FRIEND?

THEY DON'T WANT YOU HANGING OUT WITH GIRLS?
WHAT ARE THEY, FIVE?
I KNOW, EH?
NICE.
KCHAK
WHAT'S YOUR FAMILY LIKE?
I DON'T EVEN WANT TO TALK ABOUT IT.
KA-BAIL
HARSH.
DIDN'T YOU SAY YOUR MOM HAD A GUITAR?

NEW KID... UHH, YOU'RE WITH KIMBERLY, OKAY?
HI.
HI. WHAT ARE WE DOING?
IT'S SOME RETARDED PARTNER THING, AND YOU'LL PROBABLY SLACK RIGHT OFF AND I'LL END UP DOING ALL THE WORK.
UHH... NICE TO MEET YOU. I'M SCOTT.
THE PLEASURE'S ALL MINE.

WHY DO YOU WANT TO START A BAND, ANYWAY? I MEAN, OBVIOUSLY I SUCK AT GUITAR.
SCOTT! IF WE HAD A BAND, WE WOULD BE *COOL*. EVEN IF WE SUCK!
WE WOULD TRANSCEND OUR CLASS STATUS OR WHATEVER, AND BECOME AUTOMATICALLY COOL.
OUR CLASS STATUS?
YOU KNOW HOW I'M NOT A GOTH AND YOU'RE NOT A JOCK?
I'M... I'M *SUCH* A JOCK!
ANYWAY, THEY HAVE THESE-- YOU KNOW, "LUNCHA-PALOOZA"? EVERYONE GOES! WE'LL BE FAMOUS!
AND ANYWAY, WE OWN INSTRU-MENTS.
WHAT ABOUT... WELL, THERE'S ONLY TWO OF US, RIGHT?
DRUMS WOULD DEFINITELY HELP.

YOU SUCK AT DRAWING, DON'T YOU?
MAPS ARE HARD! I COULD DRAW IT REALLY GOOD IF IT WAS A SHEEP.
A SHEEP?? ARE YOU SERIOUS? DRAW ME A SHEEP!
SSIA!
I FORGET, DO SHEEP HAVE CURLY TAILS, OR IS THAT PIGS?
THAT'S THE WORST SHEEP I'VE EVER SEEN!
RUSSIA!
WHAT ARE YOU TALKING ABOUT? THIS IS SUCH A GOOD SHEEP!
RUSSIA!
YOU HANG OUT WITH THAT GIRL LISA ALL THE TIME, EH?
I GUESS.
ARE YOU GUYS, LIKE, GOING OUT?

HEY, THAT GIRL— THAT'S THE GIRL FROM MY GEOGRAPHY CLASS.
St Joel's H.S.
WHAT? WHICH ONE? THERE'S LIKE TWO ZILLION GIRLS UP THERE, DUDE.
ON DRUMS.
SHE TOTALLY CAN PLAY.
SHE TOTALLY IS HITTING THOSE DRUMS WITH THOSE STICKS, YEAH.
WELL... I'LL GET HER SOME EYELINER.

HEY, SCOTT.
OH, HI. UM, YEAH, SO, PRESENTATION ON MONDAY, RIGHT?
YEAH. DON'T WORRY, IT'LL BE FINE.
COOL. YEAH. COOL!
OH, THIS IS LAUREN. LAUREN, SCOTT. WE HAVE GEOGRAPHY TOGETHER.
HELLO.
SO, I'LL SEE YOU ON MONDAY, OKAY? FIRST PERIOD!
YEAH! FOR SURE!

I THINK I LIKE HER.
WHAT?
KIM P.
YOU LIKE HER LIKE HER? YOU BARELY EVEN KNOW HER!
UHH... I MEAN, I'D LIKE HER TO JOIN OUR BAND.
DID YOU ASK HER YET?
I'LL ASK HER ON MONDAY.

MON
ST. JOEL'S SECONDARY SCHOOL
SCOTT! OH MY GOD! THE BENVIE TECH BOYS! OH MY GOD!
THEY CAME AND BEAT EVERYONE UP!
URRRKK...
WOW! WHAT A GREAT DAY TO MISS THE BUS!

DAY

SCOTT! THEY KIDNAPPED KIM!

OUR PRESENTATION!

Benvie Tech H.S.
The BENVIE BOYS' turf!
SIMON! I'M HERE! DON'T BE A PUSSY!
WHERE IS HE? WHERE'S SIMON LEE??
URK... HE'S ON THE ROOF! BARF!
YOU'LL HAVE TO GO THROUGH ME FIRST, PILGRIM!
WHAT-EVER!

KIM!
LET HER GO, SIMON. I'VE DEFEATED ALL YOUR EVIL BOSSES.
YOU'RE FINISHED!
TOOK YOU LONG ENOUGH.
SCOTT! THIS SUCKS!

THIS IS THE BEST ST. JOEL'S COULD MUSTER?

THAT'S NOT WHAT YOUR MOM SAID LAST NIGHT!!

KRAKOW

POK

WROK
CHOKE

MERCY! PLEASE! I'VE BEEN A FOOL!
YOU'LL NEVER CHANGE.
KICK

I DIDN'T KNOW WHO'D RESCUE ME FROM THAT MANIAC, BUT I SECRETLY HOPED IT WOULD BE YOU, SCOTT.
I LIKE YOU, KIM. WE SHOULD BE DATING.
ALSO, DO YOU WANT TO PLAY DRUMS IN MY BAND?
YES, SCOTT! OH, YES!!

And so...
GOLDEN DRAGON chinesey food
D.S. BAR & SON BARRISTE
BOMB UP!!
CRAP! WHO'S BLUE?
ME! AHAHA HAHAHA HAHAHA HAHA!
THANK YOU KIM'S BASEMENT!!
HAG
WOO!

LUNCHAPALOOZA
SIGNUPS
TODAY!!
PASS THE GLITTER.
I STILL NEED IT!
No Doubt
SONIC & KNUCKLES
LUNCHAPALOOZA
THURSDAY
NOON

LUNCHAPALOOZA 9
TODAY @ NOON!
featuring:
Sonic & Knuckles!
Quentin!
Imperial otter!
Sarah Walker!
Nemesis!
ONLY $2
WE ARE SONIC & KNUCKLES! ONE TWO THREE FOUR!!
St. Joel's
LISTEN TO THIS SONG. THIS IS A REALLY GOOD SONG.

YOU'RE MOVING TO TORONTO?
ONTARIO
KEEP IT BEAUTIFUL

ARE YOU DREAMING ABOUT PLAYING VIDEO GAMES?
OH... UHH... APPAR-ENTLY.
THAT IS SO, SO PATHETIC.
ARE YOU KIDDING? YOU WOULDN'T BELIEVE HOW GREAT THIS GAME IS!

ANYWAY, QUIT DREAMING AND GET YOUR ASS OUT OF BED.
BUT... BUT IT'S NIGHT TIME!!
IT'S 11:30 A.M.! IT'S LATE!
WHAT?!
11:30 A.M. IS NOT LATE!
7
Dating a High Schooler, Part II

IT'S ALMOST NICE OUT.
YEAH, I MEAN, IT'S ABOUT TIME.
IT'S WHAT, APRIL SOME-THING?
IT'S APRIL SOMETHING, YES.
HEY, LUCAS LEE IS FILMING A NEW MOVIE HERE.
beer
NOW
SCOTT PILGRIM
HERO OF THIS BOOK
23 YEARS OLD
FUN FACT: HE WAS ALSO THE HERO OF SCOTT PILGRIM, VOLUME 1!
WALLACE WELLS
ERSTWHILE ROOMMATE OF HERO
25 YEARS OLD
FUN FACT: HE IS GAY!
WAS HE IN THAT THING "BOTTLE ROCKET" ?
WHY DO YOU CARE? IS HE HOT?
NO, THAT WAS LUKE WILSON.
NO COMMENT ON THE HOTNESS.
Not enough people are buying beer
NOW
ISN'T LUKE WILSON A GUY FROM THAT BAND I PLAYED A SHOW WITH LAST WEEK?
CAN WE TALK ABOUT SOMETHING ELSE?
Not enough people are buying beer
NOW

Not your place café
OH, YEAH, HEY, I'M INVITING RAMONA OVER FOR DINNER IN A COUPLE DAYS OR WHATEVER, SO YOU CAN FINALLY MEET HER AND STUFF.
I ALREADY MET HER, ACTUALLY.
WHAT?
YEAH, STACEY INTRODUCED US.
WHAT? WHEN?
AT YOUR SHOW.
MY SHOW?! MY SHOW WITH LUCAS LEE?!
LUKE WILSON!
WHATEVER! WHY DOES MY *SISTER* KNOW RAMONA?!

LOOK, SCOTT. I'M GOING TO ISSUE AN ULTIMATUM.
ONE OF YOUR *FAMOUS* ULTIMA-TUMS?
IT MAY LIVE IN INFAMY.
YOU HAVE TO BREAK UP WITH KNIVES. TONIGHT. YOU HAVE TO. OKAY?
BUT... BUT...
IT'S *HARD!*
IF YOU DON'T DO IT, I'M GOING TO TELL RAMONA ALL ABOUT KNIVES.
FIRST THING WHEN SHE WALKS IN THE DOOR. I SWEAR TO GOD, SCOTT.
DINGY
BUT YOU... YOU'RE...
DOUBLE STANDARD!! THESE ARE LIES! DIRTY ONES!

OH, AND I'M HAVING A FRIEND OVER TONIGHT, SO DON'T COME HOME.
WAIT!! WHAT?? WE ARE HOME! THIS IS OUR STOP!

SEE YOU TOMORROW, SCOTT.

YOU SUCK, SURPRISING NO-ONE!!!!

IF BAD WAS A BOOT, YOU'D FIT IT!!!!

YOU'RE A STUPID POO-POO HEAD!

I HAD SEXUAL RELATIONS WITH YOUR MOTHER!!!

ernet is a strange place
Don't surf alone
HEY, ARE YOU DONE SCHOOL? DO YOU WANT TO, UM, HANG OUT OR WHATEVER?
SURE! ARE YOU AT HOME?
Canada Trust
NO, I'M AT... UH, I'M AT LIKE BLOOR AND BATHURST. I'M ON A PAYPHONE.
BLOOR AND BATHURST... SOOO, WHAT ARE YOU WEARING?
WHAT KIND OF QUESTION IS THAT? *I'M* SUPPOSED TO ASK THAT! WHAT IS THIS, PHONE SEX?
PHONE SEX?? AHAHAHAHA! NO, SERIOUSLY...

SERIOUSLY *WHAT?* WHAT ARE YOU TALKING ABOUT? DO YOU WANT TO HANG OUT OR NOT?
SERIOUSLY, ARE YOU WEARING, UM, A TAN JACKET? LIKE A SPRING JACKET? AND A HOODIE?
YES...
AND A DORKY HAT!!
IT'S NOT DORKY! AND I'M SCARED! WHY ARE YOU PSYCHIC?

I'M RIGHT HERE!
OH. UH... OKAY. HI.
KNIVES CHAU
17 YEARS OLD

OOH, I NEED THIS! I CAN'T BELIEVE SOMEONE SOLD IT!
WHAT IS IT?
POP/ROCK
POP/ROCK
POP/ROCK
OP / ROCK
POP/ROCK

I LOVE THIS BAND SO MUCH! HAVE YOU HEARD THEM? THEY'RE LIKE... THEY'RE SO DEEP!
THE CLASH AT DEMONHEAD LP
CL MISC

THEY'RE FROM MONTREAL, I THINK. THEY'RE PLAYING HERE SOON, I CAN'T WAIT!

YEAH, THEY'RE OKAY.

UM... I WANTED TO INVITE YOU OVER FOR DINNER SOME-TIME.
LIKE, CHINESE FOOD?
YEAH. WELL, TO MEET MY PARENTS.
UHHH... I THINK THAT'S A REALLY BAD IDEA. LIKE, REALLY, JUST SO BAD.
NO, IT'S OKAY. WHY?
WELL... I MEAN... I'M TOO OLD FOR YOU!
NO YOU'RE NOT! MY DAD IS NINE YEARS OLDER THAN MY MOM...
POP / ROCK
AND... AND ANYWAY, ARE YOU EVEN ALLOWED TO DATE OUTSIDE YOUR RACE OR WHATEVER?
I DON'T CARE! I'M IN--

...Love!
LOVE

UM, LISTEN... I THINK WE SHOULD BREAK UP OR WHATEVER.

REALLY?

YEAH... UM... I JUST... IT'S NOT GOING TO WORK OUT.

OH...

DOES YOUR SEX DRIVE SUCK?

DOES YOUR SEX DRIVE
SUCK?
♪

WHERE'S KNIVES? NOT COMING TONIGHT?
KIM PINE
DRUMMER
23 YEARS OLD
STEPHEN STILLS
"THE TALENT"
22 YEARS OLD
YOUNG NEIL
ROOMMATE
20 YEARS OLD
OH, WE BROKE UP.
BUT MAYBE YOU'LL MEET MY *NEW* GIRLFRIEND SOON!

OH, CHECK IT OUT! I LEARNED THE BASS LINE FROM FINAL FANTASY TWO.

SCOTT, YOU ARE THE SALT OF THE EARTH.
WHAT?
OH, I'M SORRY, EXCUSE ME. I MEANT *SCUM* OF THE EARTH.

SO IT'S YOUR BIG NIGHT, EH? FAT-TENING HER UP FOR THE KILL?
GET OUT! BEGONE! ENOUGH!
HEY, COME ON. I HAVE TO EAT BEFORE SHE GETS HERE AND YOU KICK ME OUT!
STOP! HANDS OFF! NOT FOR YOU!
BUT THERE'S SO MUCH FOOD!!
THERE'S ONLY ENOUGH FOR ME AND RAMMY!
"RAMMY?" ARE YOU SERIOUSLY CALLING HER THAT?
NOT TO HER FACE.
DING DONG
SHE'S HERE! OH MY GOD, OH MY GOD!!
I'LL GET IT.

GOOD EVENING. WELCOME.
UHH... HI. WALLACE, RIGHT?
RAMONA FLOWERS
AMERICAN NINJA DELIVERY
AGE UNKNOWN
EVERYTHING UNKNOWN
FUN FACT: UNKNOWN
HEY! COME ON IN!
THANKS.
COOK
WALLACE, IT'S TIME FOR YOU TO GET YOUR COAT ON.

DO YOU MIND IF I SIT?
YOU GOT A HAIR-CUT!
ZIP
YEAH, DO YOU LIKE IT?
IT'S GOT... IT'S TWO COLOURS!
YEAH... DO YOU LIKE IT?
COOK
COOK
IT'S LOVELY. IT'S THOROUGHLY HIP.
THOROUGHLY HIP! LOVELY!
COOK

SO, DO I GET A TOUR OF THE APARTMENT?
OH, YEAH, SURE!
YOU KIDS HAVE FUN NOW!
COOK
THIS IS THE LIVING ROOM... THERE'S THE BED... YOU'VE ALREADY SEEN THE CHAIR...
WAIT... THIS IS THE ONLY ROOM?
NO NO NO. THERE'S THE BATHROOM, OF COURSE.
I... SEE.

SO ANYWAY, DINNER'S PRETTY MUCH READY. WE'VE GOT THIS SORT OF, UM, BAKED PASTA THING, I DON'T KNOW HOW TO DESCRIBE IT.
IT'S A BIT EARLY FOR ASPARAGUS, BUT IT HAS ASPARAGUS, AND IT'S KIND OF LEMONY, AND IT'S GOT A LITTLE TOO MUCH CHEESE.
IT SOUNDS GOOD. WOW. WHERE'D YOU GET IT?
OH, I MEAN, I MADE IT. I JUST DON'T EXACTLY HAVE A RECIPE SO I'M NOT REALLY SURE WHAT TO CALL IT.
YOU CAN COOK??
WELL, A LITTLE.
HOLY COW, DUDE. I THOUGHT THAT APRON WAS JUST FOR SHOW.

THIS IS REALLY GOOD. I WISH YOU HAD A TABLE, BUT THIS IS REALLY GOOD. I'M IMPRESSED.
I'M GLAD YOU LIKE IT. SORRY THERE'S NO TABLE.
I CAN'T BELIEVE YOU MADE A LOAF OF GARLIC BREAD.
GARLIC BREAD IS MY FAVOURITE FOOD. I COULD HONESTLY EAT IT FOR EVERY MEAL.
OR JUST ALL THE TIME WITHOUT EVEN STOPPING.
YOU'D GET FAT.
NO.
YOU'D GET TOTALLY FAT.
I DON'T THINK I'D GET FAT. WHY WOULD I GET FAT?
BREAD MAKES YOU FAT. *BUTTER* MAKES YOU FAT.
BREAD MAKES YOU *FAT??*

And then...
YOUR HAIR'S GETTING PRETTY LONG.

OH GOD! I NEED A HAIRCUT, DON'T I??
SCOTT'S LAST HAIRCUT
431 days ago
3 hrs before breakup
with last girlfriend
(blames breakup
largely on haircut)
HE'S BEEN CUTTING HIS OWN HAIR SINCE THEN. SOMETIMES.
WELL, I MEAN, I DON'T KNOW. IT'S CUTE LONG.
BUT IT'D BE CUTER SHORT!!! WOULDN'T IT!!!!
KRAFT
I'M JUST SAYIN'. IT'S GETTING PRETTY LONG.
IT'S CUTE. IT'S OKAY.
OH, GOD!

I KILLED HIM.
WHO?
SCOTT PILGRIM.
I GUESS HE DESERVED IT.
HAD IT COMING TO HIM.

IT'S KIND OF SAD.
SORT OF.
DO YOU DREAM ABOUT THIS KIND OF THING OFTEN?
8
The Late Scott Pilgrim

FLICK
SARA'S UNDERWEAR
TRACY'S UNDERWEAR
EMILY'S UNDERWEAR

FSSHTP
WHO THE HELL IS MAKING ALL THAT NOISE??
KIM! I KNEW IT!!!
I'M TRAGICALLY SORRY TO HAVE WOKEN YOU UP SO TRAGICALLY EARLY, SARA, AND I MEAN THAT. I REALLY DO.
WELL... WELL, GOOD! YOU SHOULD BE SORRY!

NO-ACCOUNT VIDEO
OPEN

IT'S ALMOST 11:30, SLACKER! ...AWW, YOU DIDN'T BRING ME ONE?

WHAT, A COFFEE? HOLLIE, I HAVE SOME BAD NEWS. I HATE YOU, OKAY?
YOU HATE *EVERYONE*, KIM.
YOU'RE ONE OF EVERYONE.

HAVE YOU ALWAYS BEEN THIS WAY?
WHAT WAY?
Coffee Time

LIKE, UH, A TOTALLY HATEFUL BITCH?

MAYBE I WAS A HAPPY KID.

I CAN'T EVEN IMAGINE.

NO, YOU'RE RIGHT. I WAS LIKE THIS TOTALLY SERIOUS KID, AND THIS TOTALLY ANGSTY TEENAGER.
I PROBABLY ONLY SMILED AND LAUGHED WHEN I WAS DELUDED INTO THINKING IT WOULD MAKE SOME JERK LIKE ME.

YOU'RE A HOLY TERROR, KIM, AND I'M GLAD YOU'RE ON MY SIDE.
DO YOU WANT ME TO PUT A MOVIE ON? I'M GONNA GO GET SOME COFFEE.
ADBUSTERS
die
Chicky
CHEW

OOH, CAN YOU PUT ON SOMETHING REALLY MORBID AND HORRIBLE AND JAPANESE?

NO-ACCOUNT VIDEO
OPEN
OH, GREAT, IT'S SCOTT PIGLRIM. CUE APPLAUSE.
OPEN
OH, COOL, YOU STILL WORK HERE.
WHAT ARE YOU EVEN DOING HERE? YOU KNOW ABOUT THE UNIVERSAL BAN ON YOU GUYS' ACCOUNTS.
SO I HAVE TO RENT— UM— I HAVE A LIST. HANG ON.
WHAT? WHY?
UM... LET'S SEE... OVER $1000 IN LATE FEES BETWEEN YOU AND STILLS?
I THOUGHT YOU ERASED ALL THAT!
YEAH, RIGHT! LIKE I'M WORTH A THOUSAND DOLLARS TO THIS PLACE!
NO-ACCOUNT VIDEO
ACCOUNT MANAGEMENT
MEMBER: SCOTT W. PILGRIM
BLOCKED
CURRENT FINES: $584.28
NOTES: RETURNED "THE LAND BEFORE TIME IV" 36 WEEKS LATE. HE CLAIMS THAT MICE HID THE VIDEO SOMEWHERE IN HIS APARTMENT. ALSO CLAIMS HE RENTED IT AS A JOKE. DO NOT LET HIM RENT ANYTHING. HE IS SCUM.
CLICK

CAN I RENT THESE ON YOUR ACCOUNT, THEN?
FIVE MOVIES? AS IF!
WHAT ARE THESE-- WHAT'S THE CONNECTION? *WHY*, SCOTT?
IT'S THIS DUDE. THIS GUY LUCAS LEE.
OH, RIGHT. THE ACTOR. "LET'S HOPE THERE'S A HEAVEN."
THAT WAS ACTUALLY GOOD. THE REST OF THESE ARE BAD.
WASN'T HE ON THE COVER OF *NOW* LAST WEEK? ARE YOU STALKING HIM, OR WHAT?
NO, HE'S IN TOWN, AND WALLACE FOUND OUT HE'S RAMONA'S SECOND EVIL EX-BOY-FRIEND.
CANADIAN
CUBE 2 Hyper-cube
CROC III
ZOOM
JEWEL
NIGHT MARE

SO I HAVE TO *TRAIN*, BY WATCHING THESE MOVIES, AND THEN GO FIND HIM AND FIGHT HIM.

WHAT?!
IT'S A LONG STORY, OKAY?? READ THE BOOK SOMETIME.
CUBE

ANYWAY, HE'S EVIL, AND I HAVE TO FIGHT HIM IF I WANT TO KEEP DATING RAMONA.
OH, YEAH, YOUR *NEW GIRLFRIEND*.
HOW DO YOU KNOW ALL THIS, ANYWAY? ARE YOU ACTUALLY STALKING THE GUY?
LAME LAUGHS IV
ACTION DOCTOR
MR. SHOW
BAD
WAY WORSE

WALLACE TOLD ME. WALLACE KNOWS EVERY-THING.
WALLACE WHO?
WALLACE WELLS! MY COOL GAY ROOM-MATE?
OH, RIGHT.

HOW'D YOU END UP LIVING WITH THAT GUY, ANYWAY?
I'D RATHER NOT TALK ABOUT IT.

IS IT A REALLY GAY STORY?

THE STORY IS SOMEWHAT GAY, YES.

OKAY, NEVER MIND. JUST— JUST— HOW IS LUCAS LEE EVIL?
HE'S...
DO YOU KNOW? DO YOU HAVE ANY IDEA?
YEAH, WALLACE... TOLD... ME...
YOU HAVE NO IDEA.
WHAT?
OH! OH! HE'S EVIL BECAUSE HE'S A SELLOUT!
OR... OR HE SOLD OUT BECAUSE HE'S EVIL. I FORGET.

WYCHWOOD PARK STATIONERY
SECOND CUP
NEKO CASE
WICKED
SKATEY SKATE SKATE

OKAY, I'LL HAVE...
HEY! RAMONA!

COFFEE AGENT
Stacey Pilgrim
SECOND CUP

REMEMBER ME?

HEY, STACEY!
I DIDN'T KNOW YOU WORKED HERE.
I'M FILLING IN FOR JULIE TODAY. WOW, I LOVE YOUR HAIR!

ARE YOU OKAY?
YEAH... I JUST HAD THIS WEIRD OMINOUS FEELING FOR WHATEVER REASON.
ANYWAY, HERE'S MY DOSSIER ON LUCAS LEE.
DID YOU START WATCHING THOSE MOVIES?
IF YOU TURN YOUR HEAD SLIGHTLY, YOU'LL NOTICE THAT ONE OF THEM IS PLAYING RIGHT NOW.
DON'T BE SO SURE!
OKAY, SO, LOTS OF STUFF HERE...
PRO SKATER TURNED MOVIE STAR... BLAH BLAH BLAH... YOU WOULDN'T BE INTERESTED IN THIS PART...
HE'S A SELLOUT... I ALREADY TOLD YOU THAT...

DO I HAVE TO DO ANY "SPECIAL TRAINING," OR CAN I GO BACK TO PLAYING TONY HAWK?
IT'S NOT "PLAYING," SCOTT. IT'S *TRAINING.*
OKAY, CAN I GO BACK TO *TRAINING?*
WIGU
DO FIVE HUNDRED PUSHUPS.
WHAT?! AWW... THIS SUCKS! WHAT THE HELL!
WIGU
SUCK IT UP.
I HATE TRAINING WITH YOU! YOU'RE A TERRIBLE MASTER!

I'M SO INDEFATIGABLE!!!
C'MON C'MON!!

afterwards...
HAVE YOU SEEN THE COVER OF NOW?
YES!!!
NOW
Bam! Pow! Comics aren't just for kids anymore
+
Halifax: Threat or Menace?
+
Make headlines Believe them Come back
+
Kitties are cute
The Clash at Demonhead
Montreal art-rockers make beautiful noises

I DUNNO, I THINK IT'S COOL THAT THEY'RE GETTING RECOG-NIZED.
IT'S NOT COOL!!
COME ON, MAN. AT LEAST ONE OF US MADE IT.
THWOMP
IT ISN'T OVER! WE'RE GONNA DESTROY HER STUPID PRETENTIOUS CRAPPY ART SCHOOL POSER BAND!!
DO I DETECT SOME LATENT HOSTILITY?
THEY'RE JUST GOOD, MAN. HAVE YOU HEARD THEIR CD? I'LL LEND IT TO YOU.
YOU'RE FIRED!!

I WROTE A SONG ABOUT YOU.
OH YEAH?
YEAH, IT GOES LIKE THIS... RAMONA RAMONA RAMONA RAMONA RAMONA RAMONA RAMONA!

THEN THERE'S THIS BREAKDOWN, WHICH IS KIND OF LIKE... DUN *DUN* DAAHH-NNNNININININ!
AND THEN THE SECOND VERSE GOES, *RAMONA WICKED RAMONA RAMONA RAMONA OOOOOOHHH RAMONA!*
IT'S KIND OF AN EPIC.
I CAN'T WAIT TO HEAR IT.
PHOTO STUDIO

RIIING
HELLO?
OH... HI... IS SCOTT THERE?
UH, NO... WHO'S THIS?
OH... UM... IT'S KNIVES...
OHHH, YEAH, HE'S OUT, ACTUALLY.
HE SAID HE'D BE BACK AT 8, BUT...
OHH... WELL... HE SAID WE WERE GOING TO MEET OVER THERE AND MAYBE GO OUT FOR COFFEE OR SOMETHING?
WELL, I DON'T KNOW ABOUT THAT. HE'S *REALLY* NOT HERE.
IS IT... WOULD IT BE OKAY IF I CAME OVER AND WAITED FOR HIM TO GET BACK?

WELL... I MEAN, IF YOU REALLY WANT TO, BUT I'M JUST SITTING AROUND. IT'S NOT INTERESTING. ARE YOU AT HOME?
UMM... I'M CLOSER TO YOUR PLACE...
KNIVES CHAU
17 YEARS OLD
YOU HAVE TO GO.

I'VE ONLY SEEN, LIKE, ONE OF HIS MOVIES.
"I HOPE THERE'S A HEAVEN," OR SOMETHING.
THAT ONE'S SUPPOSED TO BE GOOD, BUT IT WAS RENTED OUT.
IS THIS GOING TO BE REALLY WEIRD FOR YOU? BECAUSE, I MEAN, WE CAN DO SOMETHING ELSE IF YOU WANT.
NO, NO, IT'S COOL. I HAVEN'T EVEN SEEN HIM SINCE HIGH SCHOOL, DUDE.
I DON'T EVEN REMEMBER MY HIGH SCHOOL GIRLFRIEND.
GIRLFRIENDS.
WELL, WE CAN TURN IT OFF IF IT'S REALLY BAD.

THIS IS REALLY BAD.
I WISH YOU HAD A COUCH.

WHERE'S THE MONEY, RICARDO?! WHERE IS IT?
ME TOO.

HOW HARD CAN IT BE TO GET A COUCH?
I'VE GOTTEN COUCHES OFF THE STREET.

YOU DON'T EVEN HAVE A COUCH.
I DON'T HAVE A TV, EITHER!

WELL, I WISH YOU HAD A COUCH!

THIS IS *NOT* HOW WE DO IT IN MY *COUNTRY!*

YOUR... HEAD...

SUZETTE!
MIKEY!

THIS IS REALLY BAD.

HE'S KIND OF HOT, THOUGH.
WHAT?

LUCAS LEE? ISN'T HE?

OH, GOD... *I* THOUGHT *YOU* WERE... *DEAD!*

YOU THINK SO?

COME *ON*. *TOTALLY!*

HE DIDN'T LOOK LIKE THAT IN HIGH SCHOOL. HE WAS LIKE THIS WHINY LITTLE GREASY-HEADED SKATER.
MAYBE HE'LL GET IT ON WITH THIS CHICK SOON AND WE'LL SEE HIS BUTT.

ANYWAY, KEEP CONVINCING ME YOU'RE NOT GAY, DUDE! YOU'RE DOING GREAT!
H-HEY!
I'M NOT *DEAD*, MIKEY... BUT YOU *ARE!*
S... SUZETTE! *NO!*

HUP!
URK!
YOU'RE COOL, RAMONA. I LIKE YOU.

YOU'RE LAME, BUT I LIKE YOU ANYWAY.
TURN THE MOVIE OFF. ♡

9 As long as the road lacks perspective

HIIIIII SCOTT!
M..MOM?
HOW ARE YOU DOING? GUESS WHERE WE ARE!
UMMM... IN EUROPE?
?
GOOOOD GUESS, SCOTT!
WHAT, AM I WRONG? TELL ME I'M WRONG!
WE'RE IN ITALY. WE'RE IN ROME.
ARE THERE... ROMANS THERE?
YES, SCOTT, THERE ARE ROMANS IN ROME.
OKAY... COOL...

SO HOW ARE YOU, SCOTT? DO YOU HAVE A GIRLFRIEND?
I... UH... KIND OF?

ASK IF SHE'S CUTE!
IS SHE CUTE? DAD WANTS TO KNOW IF SHE'S CUTE.

SHE... SHE'S CUTE! YES! STOP ASKING ME ABOUT HER! I'M DONE!

HOW'S YOUR ROOMMATE? WENDELL? DOES HE HAVE A GIRLFRIEND YET?
N... NO...

HOW ABOUT A JOB? DO YOU HAVE A JOB?
I'M WORKING ON IT! I ALSO DON'T WANT TO TALK ABOUT JOBS! NEXT!

THINGS WILL START LOOKING UP FOR YOU SOON, SCOTT!
WHAT ARE YOU, A FORTUNE COOKIE?
I'M GLAD YOU HAVE A NEW GIRLFRIEND. YOU WERE SO UPSET FOR SO LONG ABOUT N--
YES, I WAS, WASN'T I! GOOD THING THAT'S ALL OVER!
DO YOU WANT TO TALK TO DAD?
YEAH! SURE! WHY NOT!

SCRTCH
HI SCOTT! DO YOU KNOW WHO THIS IS?
IS IT MY DAD?

YES! HOW DID YOU KNOW?

Scott's Ideas About Rome

I HOPE THIS IS OKAY. MY FRIENDS ARE KIND OF... I DON'T KNOW IF YOU'LL LIKE THEM.
PFFT.
THEY'RE STUPID! I HATE THEM!
AND YOU WILL TOO!
PFFT.

NO, I KNOW. GORDON DOWNIE IS A TOTALLY SWEET GENIUS.
LISTEN TO THIS PART RIGHT HERE!
HE'S A GENIUS.
HE'S *SUCH* A GENIUS.
WHO'S A GENIUS?
GORD DOWNIE. IT'S HIS SOLO ALBUM.
HE HAS TWO.
WHO'S THAT?
THE GUY FROM THE TRAGICALLY HIP.
EWWW, WHAT?

SO, WE'RE MAKING VEGAN SHEPHERD'S PIE.
SO WHO'S VEGAN?
UH... NONE OF US.
WE JUST LIKE TO BE INCLUSIVE.
I EAT FISH.
I EAT EGGS.
I EAT A LOT OF STUFF.

HEY.
HEY, KIM! THIS IS RAMONA!

RAMONA FLOWERS, KIMBERLY PINE.
HI.

HI...

HEY, KIDS! NOW YOU CAN COOK ALONG AT HOME AND IMPRESS YOUR VEGAN RELATIVES!
IF YOU'RE UNDER 23, ASK A GROWN-UP TO HELP OUT.
4 POTATOES
SOY MILK
SOY MARGARINE
RED WINE (OPTIONAL)
2 MEDIUM CARROTS
1 STICK CELERY WITH LEAVES
1 ONION
THE FINEST OLIVE OIL
KNIVES (FOR YOUR FRIENDS)
2 CLOVES GARLIC
FAKE MEAT STUFF
VEGAN GRAVY MIX
NOT PICTURED: POTS, PANS, BOWLS, ETC

SO THIS IS LIKE A COLLABORATIVE MEAL TYPE THING?
CHOPPING VEGETABLES KEEPS US OUT OF TROUBLE WITH THE LAW.
ONE! CUT THE POTATOES UP INTO SMALLISH PIECES. LEAVE THE SKINS ON IF THEY LOOK OKAY. TWO! CUT UP THE ONION, CARROT, CELERY AND GARLIC AS SMALL AS POSSIBLE. USE A FOOD PROCESSOR, OR INVITE YOUR FRIENDS AND MAKE THEM DO ALL THE WORK.
HEAD CHEF

SO LIKE... HOW DID YOU TWO MEET?
UM... IT'S KIND OF COMPLEX.
READ THE BOOK SOME-TIME.

THREE! BOIL THE POTATOES 15-20 MINUTES UNTIL TENDER, THEN MASH.
FOUR! HEAT THE OLIVE OIL IN A PAN, ADD THE VEGETABLES AND COOK FOR 15-20 MINUTES UNTIL THEY'RE VERY SOFT. ESPECIALLY THE CARROTS, WHICH ARE PROBABLY THE HARDEST.

UM... I DON'T USUALLY TELL PEOPLE THIS, BUT SCOTT AND I DATED IN HIGH SCHOOL.
WHAT? REALLY?
UH-HUH. IT'S NOT A BIG DEAL OR ANYTHING, BUT...
YOU CAN ADD SOME RED WINE. IT'S AN OPTION. IT MAKES EVERY-THING AWESOME. YOUR OTHER OPTION IS TO DRINK THE RED WINE, WHICH WORKS TOO.

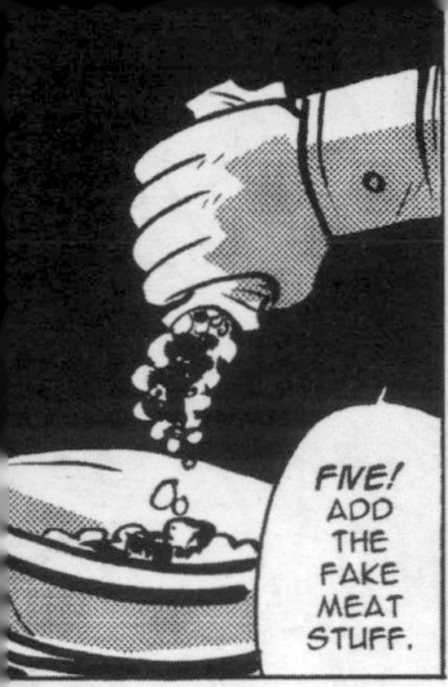
FIVE! ADD THE FAKE MEAT STUFF.

SIX! ADD THE GRAVY STUFF!

EIGHT! ADD SOME SOYMILK AND STIR SO EVERYTHING'S A BIT SAUCY!

THAT'S ALL ANCIENT HISTORY, SO DON'T WORRY ABOUT IT, RAMMY.

RAMMY? ARE YOU SERIOUSLY CALLING HER THAT?
ARE YOU SERIOUSLY CALLING ME THAT?
NO! IT WAS A JOKE! JOKE NAME! HA! HA!

NINE! MASH THE POTATOES WITH SOYMILK AND SOY MARGARINE. MMM, MASHY.

TEN! GET A 9 X 13 BAKING DISH, OR A CASSEROLE OR SOMETHING, AND GLOP THE FAKE MEAT / VEGGIE MIXTURE IN.

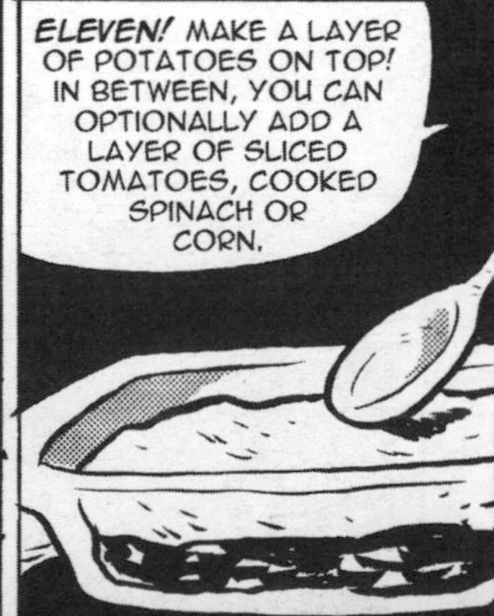
ELEVEN! MAKE A LAYER OF POTATOES ON TOP! IN BETWEEN, YOU CAN OPTIONALLY ADD A LAYER OF SLICED TOMATOES, COOKED SPINACH OR CORN.

YOU CAN SERVE IT AS IS, OR BAKE IT IN THE OVEN FOR A FEW MINUTES TO CRISP IT UP ON TOP. A SALAD ON THE SIDE WOULD BE HEALTH-CONSCIOUS, BUT WE ONLY HAVE SO MUCH ENERGY FOR THIS.
SERVE IT! WE'RE STARVING!
CORN FLAKES
MMM! IT'S GOOD!

KNIVES CHAU
17 YEARS OLD

SHOPPERS DRUG MART
TAMARA! CAN YOU MEET ME AT MY HOUSE IN LIKE, TWENTY MINUTES??

TAMARA! I'M BEING SERIOUS, TAMARA! LISTEN TO ME! I NEED TO TALK TO YOU!!
I NEED A SHOULDER TO CRY ON OR WHATEVER!

SALE 11.99
SALE 11.99

I KNOW IT'S BEEN LIKE TWO WEEKS, BUT I JUST LEARNED SOME-THING NEW! NEW INFORMATION!! DISTURBING INFORMATION, TAMARA!!!
COME ON!

OKAY, SO TWENTY MINUTES, RIGHT?

CHAU RESIDENCE
HE'S DATING SOME FAT-ASS HIPSTER CHICK!
WOW, ALREADY?

I KNOW, RIGHT?! BECAUSE I WAS WONDERING WHY HE'S BEEN TOO BUSY TO HANG OUT WITH ME ALL OF A SUDDEN!
MAYBE HE'S JUST A JERK...

HE'S NOT JUST A JERK! HE'S A REALLY SWEET GUY!
I MEAN, HE WAS GOING ON ABOUT HOW MAYBE I'M TOO YOUNG FOR HIM AND HE DOESN'T WANT TO HURT ME AND EVERYTHING, RIGHT?
BLONDY

CAN YOU READ THESE INSTRUCTIONS FOR ME? I'M SO AGITATED!
ARE YOU SERIOUSLY BLEACHING YOUR HAIR? THAT'S SO FOBBY...

SO UM, WE LET IT SIT FOR LIKE HALF AN HOUR.
HALF AN HOUR??! THIS SUCKS!
I THINK HE ONLY LIKES HER BECAUSE SHE'S OLD, YOU KNOW?
SHE'S PROBABLY LIKE 25! SHE'S SOME FAT-ASS WHITE GIRL, YOU KNOW?
I THINK YOU MENTIONED THAT SHE WAS FAT.
I DIDN'T EVEN KNOW THERE WAS GOOD MUSIC UNTIL LIKE TWO MONTHS AGO!!
SHE'S JUST SOME STUPID-- SHE'S HAD TIME, YOU KNOW?? SHE'S GOT A HEAD START! WHAT AM I SUPPOSED TO DO?? HOW DO I FIGHT THAT?
Milla Red
sexy

DO YOU THINK HE WAS TWO-TIMING YOU?
ARE YOU SERIOUS? HE WOULD NEVER!!
OH... UH... I GUESS YOU'RE RIGHT.
HE'S THE SWEETEST GUY! HE'S SO SWEET! HE REALLY CARES ABOUT MY FEELINGS, YOU KNOW?
CAN YOU OPEN THIS BOX? WE HAVE TO DO THIS ONE SOON.
GOD, I DON'T KNOW! HE MUST HAVE JUST MET HER! I MEAN, HE KNEW I WAS COOL BUT HE THOUGHT I WAS TOO YOUNG, SO HE TRIED TO FIND SOMEONE COOL BUT OLD, RIGHT?
SHE'S COOL? I THOUGHT SHE WAS FAT.
WELL, SHE *THINKS* SHE'S COOL.

IT'S SO RED! IT'S LIKE MY HEAD IS BLEEDING!!
FSSSHHH
WHAT?? DID YOU SAY YOUR HEAD IS BLEEDING?
HSSSHH
THANKS FOR HELPING ME DO THIS, TAMARA. I JUST HAD THE IDEA AND I THOUGHT, I HAVE TO DO IT RIGHT NOW! TONIGHT!
I CAN'T HEAR ANYTHING YOU'RE SAYING!
FSSSHHSHH
WHAT DO I DO? HOW DO I WIN HIM BACK? OBVIOUSLY IT'S JUST A TWIST OF FATE OR WHATEVER, ISN'T IT? STAR-CROSSED LOVERS! BORN TOO LATE! OH, GOD!!
PFFSHH
I LOOK SO, SO GOOD!!!

WHAT'S THIS WEIRD MUSIC?
THE CLASH AT DEMON-HEAD. DO YOU THINK I'M TOO YOUNG FOR HIM?
UM... YES.
BUT SHE CAN'T HAVE HIM.
YOU'RE CRAZY, KNIVES.
I'LL TAKE HER OUT OF THE PICTURE.
THIS SONG IS ACTUALLY PRETTY GOOD. WHAT DID YOU SAY THEY WERE--
THEY'RE MY FAVOURITE BAND, TAMARA! YOU CAN'T HAVE THEM!!

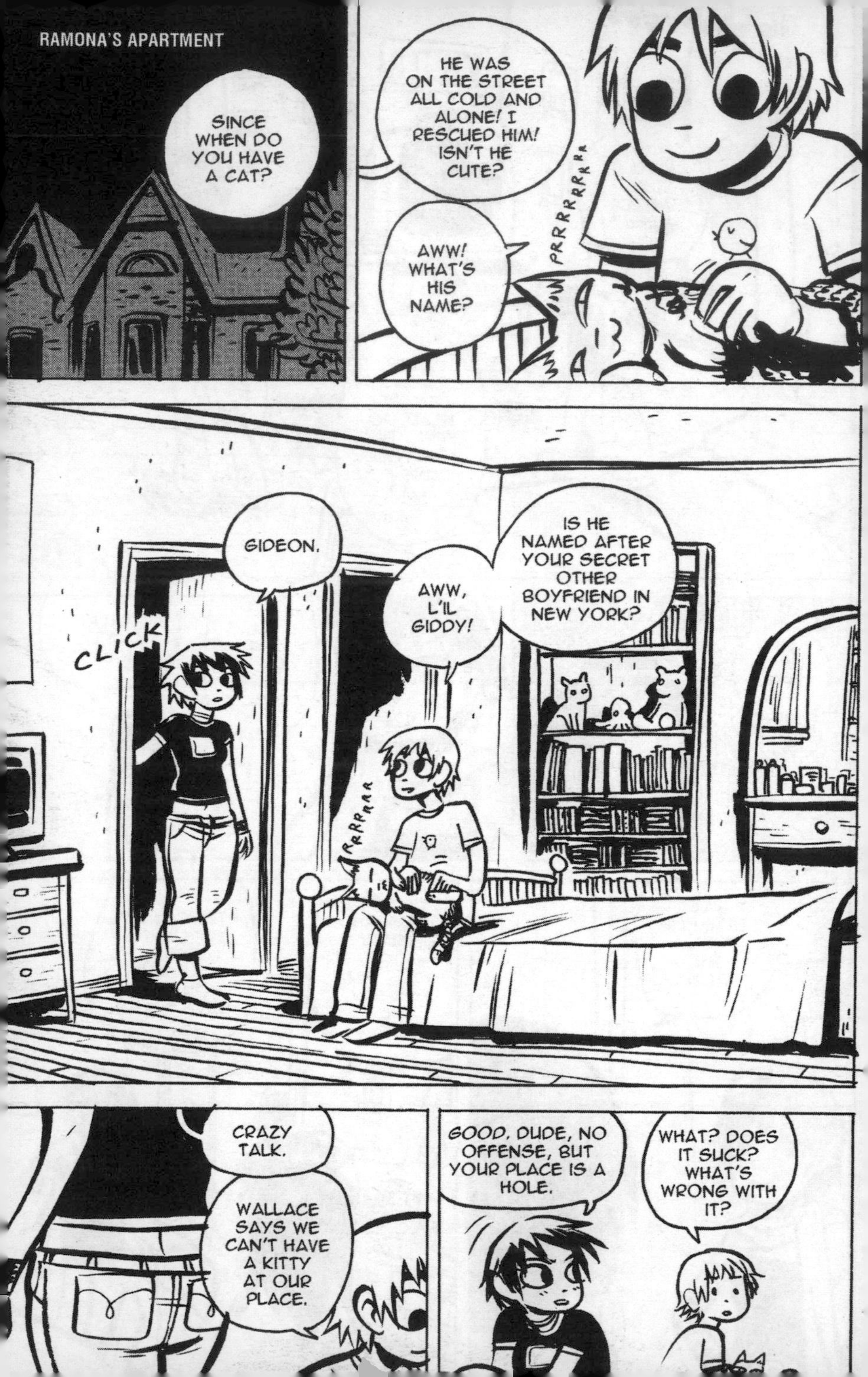
RAMONA'S APARTMENT
SINCE WHEN DO YOU HAVE A CAT?
HE WAS ON THE STREET ALL COLD AND ALONE! I RESCUED HIM! ISN'T HE CUTE?
PRRRRRRRRR
AWW! WHAT'S HIS NAME?
GIDEON.
CLICK
AWW, L'IL GIDDY!
IS HE NAMED AFTER YOUR SECRET OTHER BOYFRIEND IN NEW YORK?
RRRRRRR
CRAZY TALK.
WALLACE SAYS WE CAN'T HAVE A KITTY AT OUR PLACE.
GOOD. DUDE, NO OFFENSE, BUT YOUR PLACE IS A HOLE.
WHAT? DOES IT SUCK? WHAT'S WRONG WITH IT?

THINGS THAT ARE NOT COOL ABOUT SCOTT'S APARTMENT
1 only one room
2 only one bed and it's shared with a gay m
3 no light
Scrtch
Scrtch
THERE'S LIGHT!
2 only one bed and it's shared with a gay man
~~3 no light~~
3 no NATURAL light
4 Tiny bathroom
5 tiny kitchen
6 All items in the apartment belong to the gay man
7 Not "GIRL-FRIENDLY"

WHAT DOES "NOT GIRL-FRIENDLY" MEAN?
IT MEANS IT'S A SUCKY LITTLE HOLE IN THE GROUND, SCOTT.

AWWW...
TELL ME ABOUT LUCAS LEE, OKAY? I THINK I'M FIGHTING HIM TOMORROW OR SOMETHING.
WE WERE IN DRAMA CLASS TOGETHER IN FRESHMAN YEAR.
YOU HAD DRAMA CLASS WITH THE FUTURE ACTOR? WAS THAT AWESOME?

WELL... WAIT. IT MIGHT HAVE BEEN MATH CLASS. I JUST KNOW I REMEMBER THERE BEING A LOT OF *DRAMA*.
SO DID YOU HAVE TO FIGHT A LOT OF DUDES?
SCOTT, IT WAS THE NINTH GRADE. HE FOLLOWED ME AROUND. HE WAS A SKINNY LITTLE SNOT-NOSED BRAT.
HE ASKED ME OUT 96 TIMES AND I FINALLY SAID OKAY.

THERE WAS *SNOT* IN HIS NOSE?
WE WERE FOURTEEN OR WHATEVER. WE WERE KIDS. THERE WAS NO SEX, NO CRIME, NO GREAT HEARTBREAK OR ROMANCE.
WE SAT ON CURBS AND SMOKED.

YOU SMOKED?
YES! I SMOKED. GOD. I QUIT IN COLLEGE.
YOU SMOKED FOR YEARS?
I'M GOING TO HIT YOU SO HARD.
SO WHAT ELSE HAPPENED WITH LUCAS?
UH... NOTHING. NOTHING IMPORTANT.
I MEAN, WE BROKE UP. WE ONLY WENT OUT FOR A MONTH OR SOMETHING.
NO BIG FIGHTS OR ANYTHING? PRINCIPAL POSSESSED BY A DEMON?
NOPE.
AND I DIDN'T EVEN STRING HIM ALONG OR CHEAT ON HIM WITH ANY COCKY PRETTY BOYS.

DAMN IT! I WANTED TO GET A HAIRCUT!
GOOD JOB SLEEPING IN PAST NOON, THEN, GUY.
the next day

I LOOK LIKE A LONG-HAIRED HIPPIE!
HONESTLY, I'M NOT SEEING IT.
YOU LOOK THE SAME TO ME AS YOU'VE ALWAYS LOOKED.
HOT.

THANKS FOR WALKING DOWN WITH ME, ANYWAY. I HATE GOING TO FIGHTS ALONE. IT MAKES ME FEEL LIKE SUCH A LOSER.
I ALWAYS END UP KIND OF STANDING AROUND AND WONDERING IF I'M IN THE RIGHT PLACE AND WANTING TO GO HOME.
CASA LOMA
1 AUSTIN TERRACE, M5R 1X8
The former home of Canadian financier Sir Henry Pellatt, Canada's foremost castle is complete with decorated suites, secret passages, an 800-foot tunnel, towers, stables, and beautiful 5-acre estate gardens (open May through October).
Film shoots may be accepted subject to availability and operational requirements.
OPEN DAILY 9:30 A.M. - 5:00 P.M.
(LAST ADMISSION : 4:00 P.M.)
CLOSES AT 1:00 P.M. CHRISTMAS EVE - DECEMBER 24
CLOSED CHRISTMAS DAY - DECEMBER 25
AND THEN YOU LOSE.
NO, I NEVER LOSE.

CAN I HELP YOU GUYS?
"AHEM"
HE'S FAMOUS AND HE TALKED TO ME! ♡
EVIL. ENEMY. FIGHT. REMEMBER?

UM...
HI! LUKE
WILSON,
RIGHT?
NO,
I'M
LUCAS
LEE.

WHAT
IS THIS?
WHO
ARE
YOU?

ME?
I'M SCOTT
PILGRIM.
OH,
OKAY.
TAP
TAP

FLICK

UMM... MAYBE THIS ISN'T THE BEST TIME, BUT CAN I--
♪
THOK
HURRKKHH
SARA
GRIP
...CAN I... HAVE YOUR AUTOGRAPH?

SPINNNNN
WA-POW
WHIP

ARE YOU OKAY?
I TAKE IT WE HAVEN'T MISSED MUCH.
LET'S TAKE A BREAK, OKAY?
UGHHH

I HAVE A COOLER WITH SOME GATORADE AND BABY CARROTS AND RITZ.
THAT SOUNDS SO GOOD.

SO WHAT'S THIS MOVIE?
IT'S CALLED "YOU JUST DON'T EXIST". I'M CO-STARRING WITH WINIFRED HAILEY.
IT'S LIKE, A ROMANTIC COMEDY.
WINIFRED HAILEY? ISN'T SHE LIKE SIXTEEN?
CRUNCH
HEY, MAN, I DON'T CAST THESE THINGS!
HEH!
...IS IT GONNA SUCK?
LET'S CHANGE THE SUBJECT.

HEY, DO YOU HAVE ANY EMBARRASSING STORIES ABOUT RAMONA?
ONLY EMBARRASSING TO ME. OR HEART-BREAKING!

WHAT? WAIT, WHAT? SHE BROKE YOUR HEART? SHE DIDN'T MENTION BREAKING ANY HEARTS!
SHE LEFT ME FOR THE FIRST COCKY PRETTY BOY THAT SWAGGERED BY!
WHAT? SERIOUSLY? SHE DIDN'T MENTION ANY COCKY PRETTY BOY.
SHE DID, ACTUALLY.
THERE'S A LOT OF *THINGS* THAT RAMONA DOESN'T *MENTION*, PILGRIM.
SHE LIKES TO ACT LIKE SHE'S LITTLE MISS PERFECT, BUT THE TRUTH IS...
SHE CHEATED ON ME.
SHE *WHAT?*
SHE *CHEATED* ON ME, AND THEN DATED THAT *ASS* FOR LIKE, THE REST OF HIGH SCHOOL!
WHO DOES *THAT* REMIND YOU OF?
YOU KNOW, MAYBE SCOTT AND RAMONA ARE ACTUALLY A MATCH MADE IN HEAVEN.
DUDE, YOU'RE A GOOD ACTOR.
I'M GOING FOR AN OSCAR THIS YEAR.

THEY ALMOST DIDN'T LET ME JOIN THE LEAGUE. BUT I KNEW THEY HAD TO. I'M AN IMPORTANT FIGURE IN RAMONA'S PAST.
PLUS I'M SUPER TOUGH AND COOL.
THE LEAGUE?
DON'T TELL ME PATEL DIDN'T INTRODUCE THE LEAGUE!
UM... HE MAY HAVE. IN ONE OF HIS LETTERS. THAT I DIDN'T ACTUALLY READ.
GOD, THAT'S SO LIKE HIM!
THE *LEAGUE OF RAMONA'S EVIL EX-BOYFRIENDS*, MAN. HOW DO YOU THINK WE'RE ORGANIZED ENOUGH TO COME AFTER YOU LIKE THIS?

I... HADN'T REALLY THOUGHT ABOUT IT.
WHY ARE YOU LOOKING AT *ME*??

OKAY, LOOK. GIVE ME ALL YOUR MONEY, AND I'LL LET YOU LIVE. I'LL TELL GIDEON YOU BEAT ME UP.
WOW, YOU REALLY ARE A SELLOUT.
KISS RAMONA'S SWEET ASS GOODBYE, PILGRIM.
WAIT...
UM...
HEY...
HAVE YOU SEEN THESE STAIRS OVER HERE?

WHAT ABOUT THEM?
WELL, YOU'RE A SKATER, RIGHT? OR YOU USED TO BE?

USED TO BE?? I STILL AM! WHAT'S YOUR POINT?!
CAN YOU SHOW ME A COOL TRICK BEFORE YOU KILL ME?
WHAT, ON THE STAIRS? THERE'S LIKE 200 STEPS AND THE RAILS ARE GARBAGE!
IT'S IMPOSSIBLE.
IMPOSSIBLE?

♪

34 kph
41 kph
KINK!
OKAY... OKAY...
56 kph
KINK!
57 kph

KSH
81 kph
aaaa
WSH!
KINK!
aaa
aaa
aaaa
Noo
ooo
ooo
aaa
aaa
aa
KINK!
134 kph
309 kph

CUMULATIVE SPEED:
TOO FAST TO LIVE
AAA NOO AAA
POM
SARS

THIS SUCKS!
WHAT? WHY? YOU WIN BY DEFAULT!!
I DIDN'T GET HIS AUTOGRAPH!
YOU ARE SUCH A TOOL, SCOTT.
LOOK AT THIS MESS! GOD!!

HEY! SORRY ABOUT THAT GUY. HOW MUCH DID HE LEAVE?
LIKE... LIKE FOURTEEN BUCKS OR SOMETHING! IN COINS! WHAT A DICK!
WOW. LIFE IS HARD.
WHERE'VE YOU BEEN, ANYWAY? DIDN'T YOU WANT TO SAY HI TO THE GUY BEFORE I EXPLODED HIM?
jingle jingy
YEAHHH... NOT REALLY.
OH MY GOD, OH MY GOD!
ITEM!
WOW, LUCKY.

MITHRIL SKATEBOARD
+4 to SPEED
+3 to KICK
+1 to WILL
N-NO! I CAN'T EVEN USE THIS! WHY DIDN'T I PICK THAT SKATEBOARD PROFICIENCY BACK IN GRADE FIVE?!?
NOOOO!!!
POP
THAT WAS THE WORST FIGHT EVER!
SUCK IT UP.

TORONTO REFERENCE LIBRARY

APPROXIMATELY 82 KM OF SHELVING
CLOSE TO TWO MILLION BOOKS

MON-THU, 10:00AM-8:00PM
FRI-SAT, 10:00AM-5:00PM
SUN 1:30PM-5:00PM
CLOSED SUNDAYS ADJACENT TO PUBLIC HOLIDAYS
ALSO CLOSED SUNDAYS MAY TO THANKSGIVING

10
Nothing's ever over

KNIVES CHAU
17 YEARS OLD

WYCHWOOD PARK STATIONERY
SECOND CUP
SCOTT
AAA! NO! NOT YOU!
THANKS, SCOTT. YOU REALLY KNOW HOW TO MAKE A GIRL FEEL WANTED.
TOM COCHRANE
WHERE'S STACEY?? SHE SAID SHE WAS ON TODAY!!
YEAH, UH, SHE *WAS*, SCOTT. SHE LEFT! SHE'S DONE! IT'S LIKE 4:30!
WHAT? I THOUGHT IT WAS—WELL, WHERE'D SHE GO?
SHE WENT TO THE REFERENCE LIBRARY, WITH YOUR *FRIEND*, RAMONA FLOWERS, AND I HAVE A FEW THINGS TO SAY TO YOU ABOUT THAT, MAN!

WHAT?? THEY WENT SOMEWHERE TOGETHER?? HOW DOES STACEY KNOW RAMONA?? WHAT THE HELL IS GOING ON WITH THAT?? I TOTALLY FORGOT TO ASK!

I CAN'T BELIEVE YOU WENT AHEAD AND ASKED HER OUT, AFTER I SPECIFICALLY TOLD YOU NOT TO DO THAT!
WHAT A COMPLETE ASS! IF YOU HURT HER, SO HELP ME, I'LL—
THIS IS SO MESSED UP! HOW DO THEY KNOW EACH OTHER? AND I TOLD STACEY ABOUT—OH, MAN... I DON'T KNOW ABOUT THIS!
AND FURTHERMORE, MY BEST FRIEND, WHO YOU KNOW AS, MMM, YOUR EX-GIRLFRIEND—
WHAT!?
...WELL, SHE'S BACK IN TOWN. AND SHE WAS ASKING FOR YOUR NEW PHONE NUMBER, WHICH I WAS RELUCTANT TO GIVE OUT, FOR THE OBVIOUS REASON THAT YOU'RE A TOTAL JERKWAD, AND—ARE YOU EVEN LISTENING??

LA LA LA LA LA LA LA LA LA LA LA LA LA!
...

THIS PLACE IS
UNBELIEVABLE.

TOTAL SCIENCE FICTION. WHERE'M I SUPPOSED TO DELIVER THIS THING?
UMMM... I GUESS WE COULD TRY THE INFORMATION DESK?
Information

RIIIING
RI
PAUSE
CLICK

RAMONA?

NO!
OH. IT'S *YOU.*
YEAH, JERK! WHAT, ARE YOU SITTING BY THE PHONE LIKE A GOOD PUPPY DOG?
UNPAUSE

NO! SHE'S... SHE'S HANGING OUT WITH *STACEY!*
YOUR SISTER?
YES! GOD! YES! THEY'RE HANGING OUT! I THINK IT'S *JULIE'S* FAULT.
PEW PEW PEW

HOW COULD IT BE JULIE'S FAULT? WHAT DO YOU HAVE AGAINST JULIE??
SHE'S EVIL!
SHE ISN'T EVIL!
I SWEAR TO GOD SHE'S EVIL!
SHE ISN'T EVIL!! ANYWAY, WHAT ARE RAMONA AND STACEY DOING?
JULIE SAID THEY'RE AT THE REFERENCE LIBRARY OR WHATEVER.
WELL, WHY DON'T YOU GO AFTER THEM?
LIKE I KNOW WHERE THE REFERENCE LIBRARY IS!!
WELL... DOESN'T YOUR SISTER HAVE A CELL PHONE?
OH, YEAH, SHE DOES!
PAUSE
UHHH... DO YOU KNOW MY SISTER'S CELL PHONE NUMBER?
NO!
WELL SO MUCH FOR THAT PLAN!
UNPAUSE

Information
OKAY, GREAT, WE'RE ALL SET!
THANK YOU SO MUCH.
OH, I SHOULD TURN OFF MY CELL PHONE...
DO YOU WANT TO WALK AROUND A BIT?
YEAH... I CAN'T STAY TOO LONG, BUT I'M CURIOUS.
OKAY. WE HAVE TO GO UP IN ONE OF THESE RIDICULOUS ELEVATORS. THEY'RE RIDICULOUS.

KNIVES CHAU
17 YEARS OLD
JUST A SECOND...

GRAB
?
SNAP
SNAP

RAMONA! ARE YOU CRAZY?? YOU CAN'T JUST GO AROUND—
CLANG

WHAT IS THIS?
DID GIDEON SEND YOU?

Informa
YOU'RE DEAD, FATTY!

CLANG!
WHO ARE YOU??
I... I'VE SEEN YOU BEFORE!

THAT DAY AT THE LIBRARY...

HE...
HE WAS CHEATING ON ME!

WHAT'S SHE TALKING ABOUT?
RAMONA, ARE YOU CRAZY?? YOU CAN'T JUST TEAR UP GIANT METAL ART OBJECTS LIKE THAT!

I'LL TELL YOU WHO I AM!!!
MY NAME IS KNIVES CHAU, AND I'M A SCOTTAHOLIC!!
SHWAA

CHAU DOWN!!
DID YOU SERIOUSLY JUST SAY ALL THAT?
WSH
PTONK
HONESTLY!

HEY LARD-ASS! IF YOU WANT TO TAKE THE ELEVATOR, I CAN WAIT!!
I'LL WALK!

YOU'RE SO... SO...
...SAD!!
WHSH
DUCK
I'M SAD?
TACKLE
URK

YOU THINK YOU'RE SO COOL AND TOUGH, BUT LOOK AT YOUR FACE! I TOTALLY GRAZED YOU!!
HOW APPROPRIATE. YOU FIGHT LIKE A COW.
BUSY?? WHO DOESN'T HAVE CALL WAITING THESE DAYS?
BEEP BEEP BEEP
GASP!
NO WAY!
I'M CALLIN' THE COPS.
NO, I DON'T KNOW THE CHEAT CODE FOR SONIC 3!
I'M VERY BUSY HERE, SCOTT, WOULD YOU PLEASE STOP CALLING ME?
NO NO! WAIT! STAY ON THE LINE! MAYBE IT'LL COME TO YOU!
DON'T YOU HAVE ANYTHING BETTER TO BE DOING?

YOU THINK YOU'RE SO CUTE AND HIP!!
SHHT
JUST REMEMBER, THERE'S SOMEONE YOUNGER AND SKINNIER!!
AND SCOTT WILL REALIZE!!
GRAB
SLICE

KLONG
YOU GOT LUCKY!
I DON'T THINK I LIKE YOU.

DON'T MAKE ME CHASE YOU AROUND! I'M BUSY!
COME ON!

YOU CAN'T CATCH ME!
WHERE ARE YOU GOING NOW?
NEENER NEENER! ♪
TMP
KSH
KSH
SOMETHING TO REMEMBER ME BY!

WOK
YOU'RE UGLY AND I HATE YOU
SHE'S GONE. AND, UM... I THINK WE SHOULD LEAVE. NO OFFENSE.
WAS SHE TALKING ABOUT THE SAME SCOTT?
UMM... YEAHH... I *THINK* THEY WERE BRIEFLY DATING BEFORE HE MET YOU?
HE ALWAYS FORGETS TO TELL ME WHEN HE BREAKS UP WITH SOME-ONE...
HUH...
WHAT KIND OF IDIOT WOULD KNOWINGLY DATE A GIRL NAMED ***KNIVES?***

RIIING
RIIING
PAUSE
RII
HELLO?

HI,
SCOTT.

IT'S ME.
IT'S... IT'S YOU.
HI.
ENVY ADAMS.
HI.
HI.
IT'S BEEN A LONG TIME.
YEAH.
A YEAR, I THINK?
APPROXIMATELY.

HOW ARE YOU?
RIGHT NOW?
SURE.
NOT GOOD. I'M NOT DOING SO GOOD RIGHT NOW.
THAT SUCKS.
WELL, IT'S OBVIOUSLY YOUR FAULT.
WELL, DUH.
WELL... YEAH.
HOW'S LIFE? WHERE ARE YOU LIVING NOW?
IT'S, UM, YOU TAKE THE OSSINGTON BUS—
AND YOU'RE STILL LIVING WITH WALLACE?
YEAH. I MEAN, WE SHARE A BED. IT'S TOTALLY HOT.

UH-HUH. HOW'S YOUR LOVE LIFE? STILL BREAKING HEARTS?
WHAT? NO! STOP. I'VE BEEN—IT'S BEEN DIFFERENT. YOU HAVE NO IDEA.
PROBABLY NOT. DO YOU HAVE A GIRLFRIEND? SHOULD I BE JEALOUS?
YES. YES, YOU SHOULD. I HAVE A TOTALLY AWESOME AMERICAN NINJA GIRLFRIEND.
...
WHAT?
WHAT'S HER NAME?
I'M NOT TELLING YOU THAT!
PLEEEEASE?
IT'S... IT'S RAMONA FLOWERS.
OH.
OH? WHAT, YOU *KNOW* HER OR SOME-THING?
UH... NO.
IT SOUNDED LIKE YOU KNOW HER.
I DOUBT THAT VERY MUCH.

WELL... SHE'S MY GIRLFRIEND.

...

WHAT?

I'M JEALOUS.
YOU'RE JEALOUS?

I'M ALLOWED.
YOU LEFT ME! FOR... FOR THAT COCKY PRETTY BOY!

YOU'VE NEVER EVEN SEEN HIM.
YEAH, I KNOW.

YOU LEFT ME FOR A GUY I'VE NEVER EVEN SEEN.

WELL...

MAYBE YOU'LL SEE HIM SOON.

OH RIGHT.
SO WHAT IS THIS? WHY ARE YOU CALLING, ENVY?
WHAT'S THAT SUPPOSED TO MEAN?
IT MEANS ARE YOU EVIL, OR ARE YOU JUST BEING NICE?
WHAT, LIKE DO I HAVE ULTERIOR MOTIVES OR SOMETHING? AM I A USER?
YOU'RE SUCH A USER! IT'S NOT LIKE I HAVE TO ASK!
OKAY, I'M KIND OF A USER. WE'RE PLAYING A FEW SHOWS AT LEE'S PALACE THIS WEEKEND, AND WE'RE GETTING SOME LOCAL BANDS TO OPEN—
YEAH?
...AND THIS ONE OPENING BAND FOR SUNDAY GOT IN A BIG FIGHT AND DROPPED OUT—
YEAH?
YEAH, THE LEAD GUITARIST AND BASS PLAYER WERE DATING AND THEY BROKE UP AND EVERYTHING KIND OF CRUMBLED—
YEAH?
YEAH, AND I THINK THEIR DRUMMER IS IN LIKE A COMA—
THE DEMON
YEAH, AND?
...AND I WAS HOPING YOUR BAND COULD PLAY.

OH.
OH?
YEAH. OH.
COME ON. THIS IS SUPPOSED TO BE A BIG DEAL.
I'M A PITY CASE.
GIVE ME A BREAK. YOU AND STEPHEN HAVE A NEW BAND, RIGHT?
SEX BOMB OR SOME- THING, RIGHT?
SEX BOB- OMB.
RIGHT. SO LOOK, I'M PUTTING YOU GUYS ON THE GUEST LIST FOR FRIDAY, OKAY? SO COME SEE US AND WE'LL TALK AFTERWARDS, OKAY?
...OKAY.
IT'S BEEN NICE CHATTING WITH YOU.
UH- HUH.
I'M GLAD WE HAD THIS LITTLE TALK.
SURE.
CLICK

URRGGHL.
ARE YOU OKAY?
ARE YOU SICK? FOOD POISONING?
...

WAS YOUR POOP A WEIRD COLOUR? LIKE, UHH... GREY?
...
UMM... DID YOU FIND OUT ABOUT HOW I ACCIDENTALLY SAVED OVER YOUR GAME IN FINAL FANTASY? NO, LAST TIME THAT HAPPENED YOU WERE TOTALLY *CRYING*, SO—
OH, GEEZ, DID RAMONA DUMP YOU? I'M SO SORRY—
...
NNN
NO?

ENNNNN
EN...
ENVY?
ENVY CALLED?

SHIT.

11

Things Keep Happening

HEY.
SCOTT? WHAT'S UP?
CHOP CHOP
UHHH... I DON'T KNOW.
WHAT'S WRONG??
SHE...
OH MY GOD, DID RAMONA BREAK UP WITH YOU BECAUSE OF THAT CHINESE GIRL???
NO! ENVY CALLED—WAIT, WHAT? WHAT ABOUT RAMONA?
SHE CALLED? WHAT, JUST TO DESTROY YOUR SOUL???
WHAT DID YOU SAY ABOUT RAMONA?
I'VE BEEN MEANING TO ASK, HOW THE HELL DO YOU KNOW RAMONA, ANYWAY?

I DON'T KNOW!! IT JUST HAPPENED!!! SHE KEEPS COMING TO THE SECOND CUP!! I DIDN'T EVEN *KNOW* YOU GUYS WERE DATING--
DID YOU TELL HER ABOUT KNIVES?? KNIVES IS *OVER*, OKAY?!
I DIDN'T *TELL* HER, EXACTLY...
WHAT? WHAT HAPPENED?
A SEVENTEEN-YEAR-OLD CHINESE GIRL FLEW DOWN FROM THE TOP OF THE ELEVATORS AND RAMONA DEFLECTED HER WITH A PIECE OF CORPORATE ART AND THEN THEY FOUGHT FOR A FEW MINUTES AND THEN THE GIRL LEFT.
WHAT??! THEY FOUGHT!?!
YES!!
AND I *MISSED IT?!?*
AAAAA OHHHHH EEEEE
UM... SORRY. I SPILLED MY HOT COCOA.
SO... UH...
IS SHE GOING TO DUMP ME NOW?

I HAVE SOME BAD NEWS.
WHAT, YOU BROKE UP WITH YOUR NEW GIRLFRIEND, BUT SOON WE'LL MEET YOUR *NEW* NEW GIRLFRIEND?
PAUSE
NO, UH... ENVY ADAMS ASKED US TO PLAY A SHOW.
WE HAVE TO GO MEET HER TOMORROW AND TALK ABOUT IT.
OR WHATEVER.
THAT'S BAD NEWS??
THAT'S *GREAT* NEWS!!

...YOUR EX-GIRL-FRIEND?
WE'RE GONNA OPEN FOR THEM? THEY'RE KNOWN!
WE COULD GET KNOWN!!
YEAH, AT LEE'S PALACE.
I SAW HER ON THE COVER OF NOW.
I'VE SEEN ALL MY FAVOURITE BANDS PLAY THERE!!
I USED TO SEE A LOT OF SHOWS THERE.
SHE'S PRETTY.
WE SUCK!! OH MY GOD!! WE'RE SO BAD!! WE CAN'T PLAY THIS SHOW!
WE... WE DON'T SUCK. I MEAN... I GUESS.
WE DO KIND OF SUCK. KIND OF BADLY.
CALL HER AND CANCEL, OKAY?? SERIOUSLY.

Friday...
IT'S THE FIRST REAL T-SHIRT DAY OF THE YEAR!
AND YET NEITHER OF US IS WEARING A T-SHIRT.

POO ON YOU. I'M HAPPY! AND YOU LOOK GOOD.
THANKS...

SIGH
OH, WOULD YOU STOP!

SO. YOUR EX-GIRLFRIEND'S BAND.
YEP.

BALL AND HOCKEY PLAYING PROHIBITED
WHAT'S HER NAME AGAIN?

ENVY ADAMS.

REALLY?

WELL, SORT OF. HER INITIALS ARE *N* AND *V*, SO...

ENVY. THAT MAKES SENSE. THAT'S A DECENT BASIS FOR A NICKNAME.
I GUESS. STEPHEN STILLS MADE IT UP, I THINK.

MY INITIALS ARE *R.V.*, SO MY NICKNAME COULD BE TRAILER GIRL. GET IT?
THE V IS FOR VICTORIA.

OH, LIKE THE QUEEN?
OH YEAH, YOU GUYS STILL WORSHIP THE QUEEN OR WHATEVER, DON'T YOU!

UHHH... NOT THE ONE THAT DIED A HUNDRED YEARS AGO, NO.
OOH, GO AHEAD AND POKE FUN AT MY POOR QUEENOLOGY, CANADA BOY.

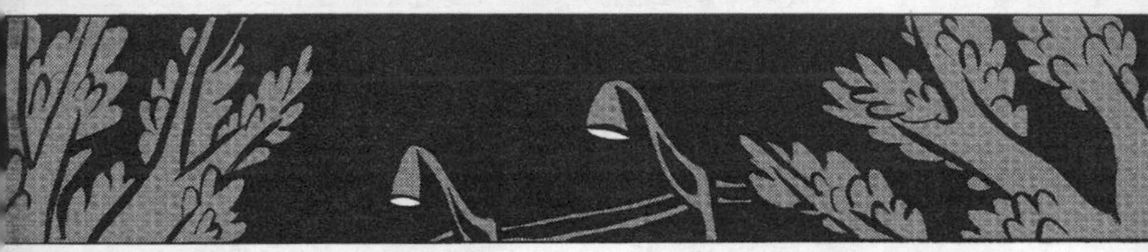

SO, UMMM... DO YOU HATE ME NOW?

WHAT? AM I ACTING LIKE I HATE YOU?
NOT YET...

I DON'T HATE YOU. HEY, TELL ME HOW YOU BROKE UP WITH ENVY ADAMS.

I... WELL, IT'S COMPLI-CATED.
DON'T YOU WANT TO HEAR ABOUT HOW WE GOT TOGETHER AND EVERYTHING? WE MET AT THE START OF UNIVERSITY--

EWWW! NEW GIRLFRIENDS ONLY WANT TO HEAR BAD STUFF ABOUT EX-GIRL-FRIENDS, DUDE, COME ON.
OH. WELL, WE BROKE UP ON NEW YEAR'S EVE. A YEAR AGO. OVER A YEAR AGO.

WERE YOU WASTED?

NO, I DON'T DRINK.

OH RIGHT.
SO DID SHE GIVE YOU A REASON?
WELL... SHE WANTED TO MOVE TO MONTREAL BECAUSE SHE MISSED HER BEST FRIEND, THIS GUY TODD OR SOMETHING.

AND TWO WEEKS LATER, YOU HEARD THEY WERE SLEEPING TOGETHER, I GUESS?
BASICALLY.

I DATED A TODD ONCE.
GREAT STORY! MAYBE IT WAS THE SAME GUY!

JERK. WHAT'D YOU DO AFTER THAT?
I...
I DON'T REMEMBER.
PUNCH!

BULL!

MY MEMORY OF THAT YEAR IS HAZY. I SWEAR TO GOD. VERY HAZY.
AS IF! DID YOU GRADUATE?

I DON'T REMEMBER.
WHAT EVER!!!

SO AFTER THAT, THE FIRST REAL MEMORY I HAVE IS, THERE WAS THIS RESTAURANT THAT OPENED WAY OUT ON QUEEN WEST—

YOU REMEMBER SOME RESTAURANT BETTER THAN YOUR LAST YEAR OF COLLEGE??

LET ME TELL YOU ABOUT THIS PLACE, OKAY?
IT WAS THIS LIKE, NOUVEAU-MEXICAN PLACE, CALLED THE GILDED PALACE OF FLYING BURRITOS. THEY SERVED THE MOST AMAZING GIGANTIC DELICIOUS BURRITOS AND ALL THIS FANCY TEX MEX TYPE STUFF.
AND ALL THE SERVERS WORE THESE AWESOME NUDIE SUITS, AND THE GIRLS WORE LIKE THESE COW-GIRL OUTFITS—
OKAY, STOP. IT SOUNDS RETARDED. YOU SOUND RETARDED. I'M BREAKING UP WITH YOU.
...AND IT WAS MY FAVOURITE RESTAURANT AND I ATE THERE LIKE FIVE TIMES A WEEK AND I TRIED TO GET A JOB THERE FOR MONTHS AND THEN I FINALLY DID!
YOU'RE TOTALLY MAKING THIS UP.

FREE FOOD! MY FAVOURITE FOOD, *FREE!*
AND A *WEEK* AFTER I GOT THE JOB, LITERALLY SEVEN DAYS, THE PLACE GOT SHUT DOWN BY THE D.O.J. FOR SELLING DRUGS, OR MONEY LAUNDERING, OR SOME OTHER BAD TYPE OF THING!
NOTICE
YOU ARE FIRED
WELL... THAT SUCKS. IF IT'S TRUE. WHICH IT'S NOT.
YEAH, SO THEN I PLUNGED BACK INTO DEPRESSION, BASICALLY. I WROTE A SONG ABOUT IT. IT'S LIKE THIS SAD COUNTRY WALTZ...
CIBC

Untitled Composition by Scott Pilgrim
3/4, mournful
G D G
The Gilded Palace of Flying Burritos
G D
Excellent Nouveau Mexican Cuisine
G C D
We all got to wear Swank-Ass Nudie Suits
G D G
I shoulda known it was a lousy pipe dream
C G D G
Ohhh, ohhh, what an awesome job
C G D
Ohhhh, ohh, what do I do now??
C G Bm Em
Ohhh, ohhhhh, it's like I've been robbed
G
Spent the last of my paycheque
D G
And I'm feelin' pretty downnnnnn!!

LEE'S
PALACE
WHEN I TELL YOU ABOUT MY LAST JOB, IT'LL BE SUCH A BETTER STORY.
GOD, WHAT IS THIS? THEY'RE LIKE SOME BIG THING ALL OF A SUDDEN!

STP

YO!

HEY. HAVE YOU SEEN HER YET?
NOPE.
DUDE. NICE HAIR.

STEPHEN STILLS, YOU GOT A *HAIRCUT?*
YES! SHUT UP!

WHY DON'T I HAVE A HAIRCUT YET? WHY DO *YOU* GET A HAIRCUT?
I WAS NERVOUS! SHUT UP!
DUDE, WE'RE JUST *TALKING* TO HER! IF ANYONE SHOULD BE NERVOUS, IT'S OBVIOUSLY--

I KNOW! SHUT UP!
--OH MY *GOD!* LOOK AT KIM!
KIM'S WEARING *HIGH HEELS!*

WHATEVER. LOOK WHO NEIL'S HERE WITH.
KNIVES CHAU
17 YEARS OLD
WHAT THE HELL?!

SHE'S VERY, UH... ADAPT-ABLE.
DID SHE SEDUCE NEIL?

SO YOU DATED HER BRIEFLY?
VERY BRIEFLY!

I BET NEIL WILL DATE HER EVEN BRIEFLY-ER.
I CAN'T BELIEVE THIS!

SHOULD WE TAKE HIM OUT BACK AND BEAT HIM UP?

HEY, KIM!

HEY. I DIDN'T KNOW YOU GUYS WERE COMING TO THIS.

WELL, THEIR FIRST EP WAS OKAY. I HAVEN'T HEARD THE ALBUM YET.

JOSEPH
HER ROOMMATE
24 YEARS OLD
HOLLIE
COWORKER
26 YEARS OLD

BUT THE *REAL REASON* WE'RE HERE IS BECAUSE JOSEPH HAS A CRUSH ON THEIR BASS PLAYER.

I HAVEN'T SEEN HIM. IS HE HOT?
I DON'T KNOW. IS HE HOT, JOSEPH?

HE IS AS HOT AS THE FLAMES OF THE HELL YOU BITCHES ARE GOING TO.

I WAS IN MONTREAL IN FEBRUARY AND WE HUNG OUT A LITTLE.
HOW DID SHE LOOK?
MONIQUE
OLD CLASSMATE
23 YEARS OLD
SANDRA
SAME DEAL
24 YEARS OLD

REALLY GOOD. REEEALLY GOOD.

DID YOU GIRLS HAVE ANY OTHER CONVERSATIONAL TOPICS IN MIND WHEN YOU CAME OVER TO TALK TO US?

WELL, ARE YOU GOING TO INTRODUCE US?
UHH... THIS IS RAMONA. I THOUGHT YOU KNEW HER.
YEAH, DIDN'T WE MEET AT THAT PARTY THAT ONE TIME?

I GUESS.
SO ARE YOU GUYS AN ITEM NOW?

ARE WE AN ITEM?
I'M SORRY, WHAT?

DUDE.
HI, STEPHEN! I LIKE YOUR HAIRCUT!
OH... UH... HI. THANKS.

I CAN'T *WAIT* TO SEE THEM PLAY! ARE YOU EXCITED? ARE YOU A BIG FAN?

THEY'RE OKAY...

I CAN'T WAIT TO SEE *HER* IN PERSON! SHE'S *SO* COOL.
I HAVEN'T SEEN HER IN A WHILE.

WAIT... WHAT... YOU *KNOW* HER?

WE... YEAH.
I USED TO BE IN A BAND WITH HER. SHE USED TO DATE SCOTT.

SO, WE THINK YOU GUYS SHOULD COME UP FRONT AND... UH... DANCE...

OH, GOD.
IT'S THAT STUPID BITCH SARA.
SO I'M ALL, OH MY GOD, AND SHE'S ALL—
WHO?
ONE OF MY IDIOT ROOM-MATES. HIDE ME.
YOU DISLIKE SOMEONE? HOW UN-USUAL!

OH, GOD. IT'S THAT STUPID BITCH KIM.
SARA
KIM'S ROOMMATE
AGE: WHO CARES
I DON'T KNOW THIS GIRL
WHO?
THAT ROOMMATE WE ALL DESPISE.

THIS BAND SUCKS.
SHIMMY SHIMMY SHIM-MAYYY!
THAT'S WHAT THEY'LL BE SAYING ABOUT *YOU* ON SUNDAY.
AT LEAST I... WAIT... SOME-THING... YOU... INSULT...
SCOTT, THAT WAS *NOT* A GOOD COMEBACK.
THAT WAS ACTUALLY NOT BAD FOR SCOTT.

HEY, SO I HEAR YOU GUYS ARE OPENING ON SUNDAY TOO...
OH, HEY. YEAH.
CRASH & the boys
I ♥ ZACH BRAFF

SO WE WERE HOPING WE COULD PLAY FIRST, AND YOU GUYS SECOND...
ARE YOU... LUCAS LEE?
NO, I'M LUKE WILSON.

YOU SEE THAT GIRL?

WITH THE GLASSES?
NO. YEAH. WAIT... YEAH.

ISN'T SHE THE DEMONHEADS' DRUMMER?
TOTALLY.

FLIC

OH MY GOD, SHE *SMOKES!*
OH MY GOD, SHE'S ***EVIL!***

PRETTY HOT, THOUGH.
TOTALLY.

and then it was time...
WOO!
I WANT TO GO HOME.
SHH.
and then

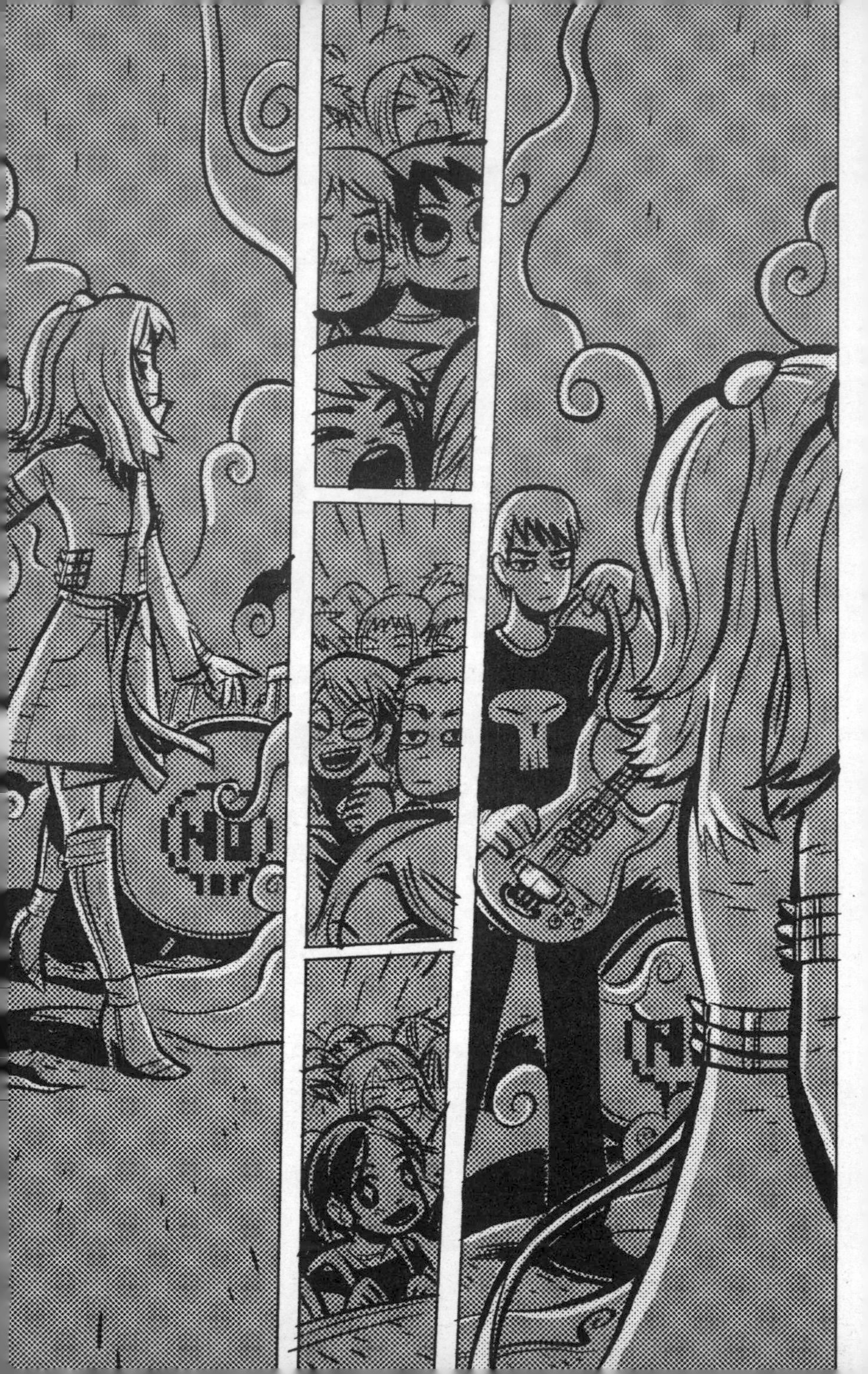

SO, UH, THAT'S HER!
BUT WHAT?
I FIGURED! BUT—
THAT GUY ON THE BASS, TODD??
HI, TORONTO! THANKS SO MUCH FOR COMING! THIS IS CALLED "UNDER WATER MOTOR SCOOTER!"
YEAH??
THIS GUY
moog
KORG

HE REALLY IS THE SAME TODD I DATED!!
...MY THIRD EVIL EX-BOY-FRIEND!!
next: scott pilgrim & the infinite sadness!

ooh-malley... – Peacefully, passed away in his 90th year after a brief battle with cancer on Wednesday, January 19, 2005 at Mt. Sinai Hospital. Beloved father of Barbara, cherished grandfather of Stacey and Jennifer, and dear great-grandfather of Stacyanna and Jayden. Brother of Mary Pagon.

Portrait of the author by **Joel MacMillan**

THE AUTHOR'S DETAILS

Bryan Lee O'Malley was born in London, Ontario. His only goal in life was to become rich. At the time of this writing, he is not very rich at all. The *Scott Pilgrim* series is his life's work, after which he plans to retire to a house by the ocean and eat smoked salmon for every meal until his death. He currently lives in an apartment somewhere in Canada with **Hope Larson** and two cats.

www.4thestate.co.uk* | *www.scottpilgrim.com* | *www.radiomaru.com